To our family,
You are life's greatest blessing.
We love you!

# SCHOOL IS DIFFERENT THIS YEAR AND THAT'S OK!

It's been a nice, long summer. The animals are starting to think about going back to school.

Last spring, everyone had to do remote-learning because of a bad virus called COVID-19, or Coronavirus. This virus can make people very sick. Staying at home helped to keep everyone safe.

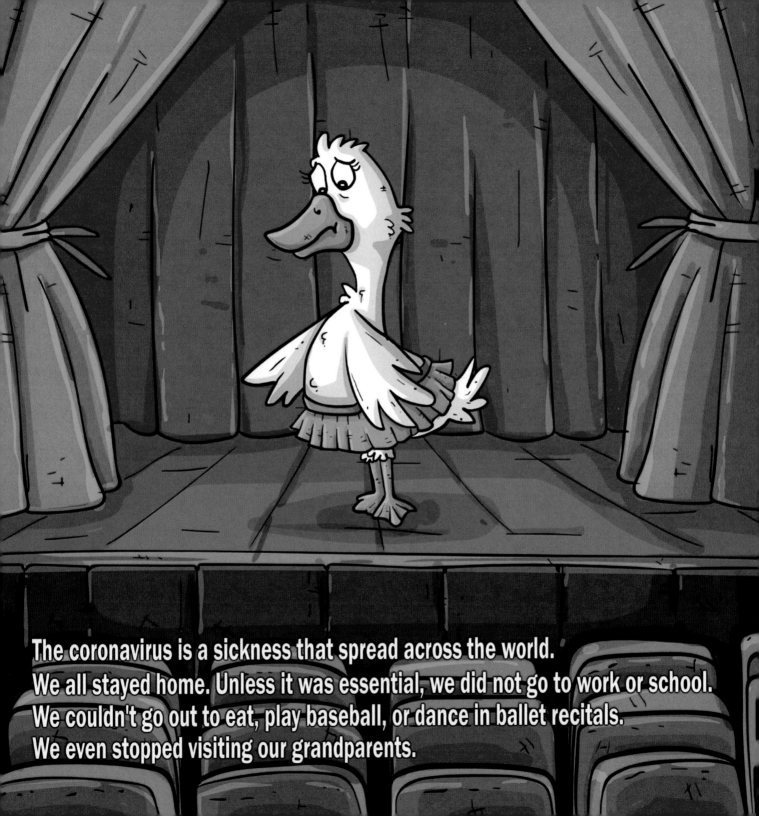

The coronavirus is a sickness that spread across the world.
We all stayed home. Unless it was essential, we did not go to work or school.
We couldn't go out to eat, play baseball, or dance in ballet recitals.
We even stopped visiting our grandparents.

Lorenzo and Gracie will do remote-learning this fall.
Lorenzo is excited! He thought it was a lot of fun.
He got to see his friends on the computer,
eat snacks all day, sleep-in,
discover new ways to learn,
and spend more time with his family.

Gracie didn't like remote-learning. She missed her friends and her teacher... A LOT.
School at home was boring without fun chairs, recess, and art.
There was a lot of time on the computer doing videos and this was hard for Gracie.
She wanted to go back to school. She just wanted her Mom to be her Mom
and not her teacher too.

The Goat family is going to school in-person. This is ok too. Johnny doesn't really care which option, but he does want to play baseball again.

Paisley is worried. She's heard a lot of grown-ups talking about it. She's not so sure about wearing a mask and not picking her seat at lunch. The classrooms look different too. Everything is SOOOO far apart.

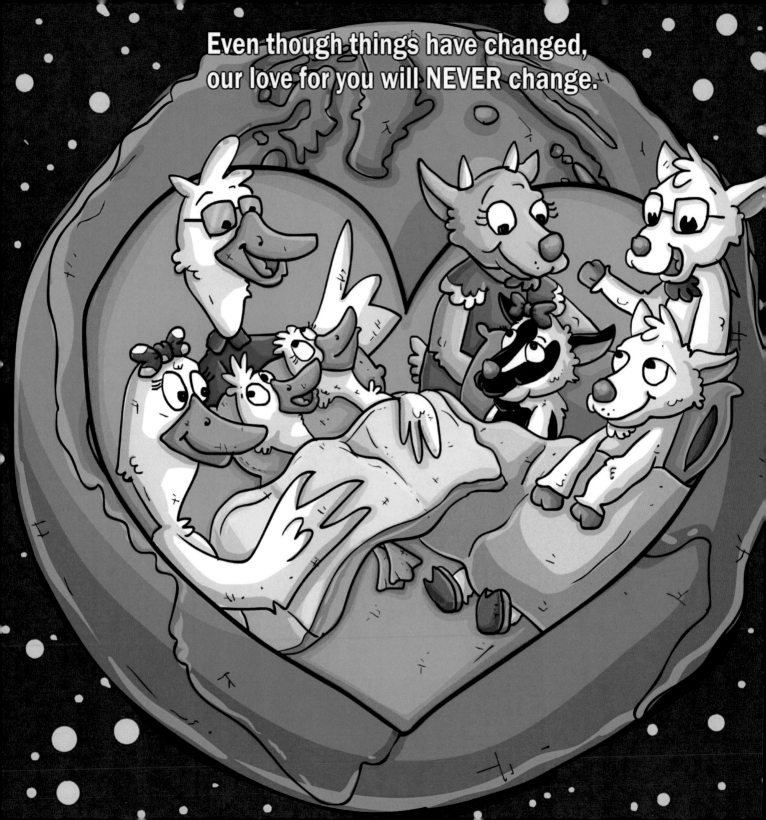

If you are at home, in school, or somewhere in between, we are all in this together. School is different this year and that's ok!

Made in the USA
Monee, IL
14 April 2021